Who's Been in Our Tree?

Diana Batchelor

D1634758

915 00000232937

Pssst. Hey grown-ups! There is a section just for you at the end of the book, called Things to Talk About.

This story will entertain children, introduce them to a range of different reactions to crime, and help them talk about feelings. If they have experienced something that has upset or worried them, this book will reassure them that they're not alone. At the end of the book you will find activities for children and tips for grown-ups that will give you the tools and confidence you need to help them.

Copyright © 2017 Diana Batchelor

The moral right of the author has been asserted.

Apart from any fair dealing for the purposes of research or private study, or criticism or review, as permitted under the Copyright, Designs and Patents Act 1988, this publication may only be reproduced, stored or transmitted, in any form or by any means, with the prior permission in writing of the publishers, or in the case of reprographic reproduction in accordance with the terms of licences issued by the Copyright Licensing Agency. Enquiries reproduction outside those terms should be sent to the publishers.

LEWISHAM LIBRARY SERVICE	
915 00000232937	
Askews & Holts	27-Sep-2019
JF	£6.99
	LWLEW

Matador
9 Priory Business Park,
Wistow Road, Kibworth Beauchamp,
Leicestershire. LE8 0RX
Tel: 0116 279 2299
Email: books@troubador.co.uk
Web: www.troubador.co.uk/matador
Twitter: @matadorbooks

ISBN 978 1788033 589

British Library Cataloguing in Publication Data.
ogue record for this book is available from the British Library.

Printed and bound by CPI Group (UK) Ltd, Croydon, CR0 4YY
Typeset in 20pt Chelsea Market by Troubador Publishing Ltd, Leicester, UK

Matador is an imprint of Troubador Publishing Ltd

MIX
Paper from
responsible sources
FSC® C013604

With thanks to...

M, who asked for a story when I was supporting him in the aftermath of a burglary.

Dr Fiona Snyder, a Clinical Psychologist working with children and young people in Sussex and Kent. Her expertise ensured that this book offers evidence-based practical advice that children and families can rely on.

The many children, parents, teachers and youth practitioners who gave me encouraging and constructive feedback through You & Co.

Alice Harman, an experienced children's editor, for her hard work and guidance in bringing this book to print. Sue Foster, for illustration advice; and Jonathan Smith, for being in my corner.

Fox peeked inside the doorway.

He wasn't sure what had happened.
Everything in the tree was upside down.

'Let me through!' yelled Badger, scrambling past. 'I want to see too.'

But then she stopped, shocked.

'There are empty spaces where our things used to be,' groaned Squirrel.

Hedgehog counted them:

One, the shelf where the TV used to be.

Two, the table where the games used to be.

Three, the cupboard where the bag of Favourite Things used to be.

'Someone has been in our tree,'
sniffled Fox.

And this is what happened next:

Fox's knees went all wobbly.

Hedgehog curled up
into a ball.

Squirrel was frozen to the spot.

Badger's heart was beating really fast. She thought it was going to pop.

Badger called the Birds and told them what happened.

The Birds asked lots of questions and hopped around looking for clues.

'Don't worry,' they chirped. 'It's our job to catch whoever has burgled your tree.'
And they flew away into the forest.

The four friends tidied up the mess in the tree.
Then they waited until they felt better.

But more strange things started to happen...

At night time Badger couldn't sleep because the burglars kept going round and round in her head.

And at school she couldn't concentrate.

Fox didn't want to be by himself.
Wherever the others went, he went too.

Even at night.

Hedgehog felt angry all the time.

She shouted at the others when things went wrong.

She even shouted when things went right.

Squirrel was very jumpy.

He jumped when a door slammed.

He jumped when the tree creaked.

He even jumped when the wind blew.

One day, the four friends
were talking.

'I wish it never happened,'
Squirrel squeaked.

'I wonder why the burglars chose our tree?'
Badger grunted.

'I wish we could get our things back,'
Hedgehog sighed.

'I have an idea!' cried Fox.

'We can't undo what happened,
but maybe we can undo some
of these strange things.

Let's all make a plan.'

And that's exactly what they did.

Fox's Plan

Badger's Plan

one two three four five six seven eight nine ten

Hedgehog's Plan

When I feel like shouting, I'll try counting to ten.

And I'll go to football more often so I can do all my running and shouting there.

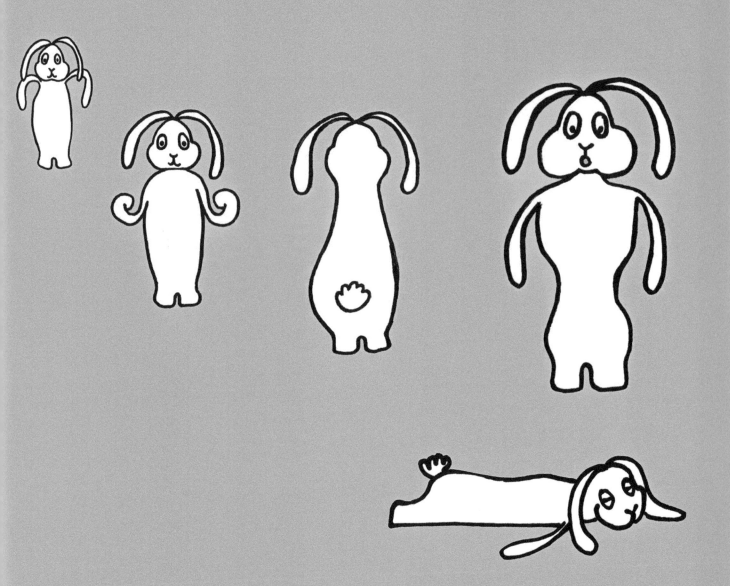

Squirrel's Plan

When I feel jumpy, my friend will teach me how to do the Flippety Floppety Rabbit to relax!

I scrunch up each part of my body, then let it flop like a flippety floppety rabbit!

They started on the plan straight away.

On the first day, the strange things
were still happening.

On the second day, too.

On the third day Badger said,
'Last night the burglars were still in my
head, but this time they weren't so scary.'

On the fourth day, some of the strange things happened again.

But on the fifth day Fox said, 'I'm going to sleep in my own room tonight!'

Some days they felt better, other days they felt worse. But, little by little, the plan was working.

The Birds came back to say they couldn't find the burglars.

'Did you find our television and games?' Hedgehog asked.

'No, we're so sorry,' tweeted the Birds, 'and we couldn't find your bag of Favourite Things either. What was inside?'

'Inside,' said Hedgehog, 'there were
all sorts of feelings and memories.
There was happiness and laughter
and fun. And now they've all been stolen.'

Just then, Squirrel spied a piece
of string sticking out from under
a chair. 'What's that?' she squealed.

'It's still here!' whooped Badger.
'It was here all along!'

Fox stared at the bag and
whispered, 'It's even bigger
than before...'

FAVOURITE THINGS

All the old feelings and memories were still inside, but now there were all sorts of new ones too!

Some made them feel bad –
like jumpiness and shouting
and being scared.

But some made them feel
good – like planning and playing
football and learning how to relax.

The shelf where the
television used to
be was still empty.

The table where the
games used to be
was still empty.

'But we still have all our
feelings and memories,'
said Badger, 'and they
can never be stolen.'

'If they can't be stolen,'
said Fox with a twinkle in
his eye, 'we don't need to
keep them tied up in a bag.'

So they let them out.

The End

What about me?

You've read the story, now it's your turn!

How do you feel?
Look back at the first pages of the story
and talk to someone about what
happened and how you feel.

Favourite Things
Copy the picture of the bag opposite.
Write or draw the things you have that
can't be stolen.

Making your plan
To make your own plan, read the questions
on the next two pages and write or draw
what you decide to do.

My plan

Are you worried when you're on your own? What makes you feel better? Put it in your plan! Who will you talk to about your feelings?

Do you think or dream about what happened? Can you draw it, then change it into something less scary?

Have you had trouble at school? Think of an adult who you can tell.

Have you been feeling angry or grumpy? Can you take deep breaths or count to ten like Hedgehog? How can you let your anger out? What about sport or something else that takes a lot of energy?

Have you been feeling jumpy or scared? What makes you feel safe and happy? Put that thing or person on your plan! Can you do the Flippety Floppety Rabbit?

Is there anything you want to find out from an adult, or from the police? Who will you ask?

Do the Flippety Floppety Rabbit

Scrunch up your
face so it's all wrinkly.
Keep it scrunched for a moment...
Then let it go flop, like
a flippety floppety rabbit.

Lift up your shoulders very, very
high. Keep them lifted for a moment...
Then let them go flop, like a
flippety floppety rabbit.

Imagine you're squeezing
two carrots in your hands
as tight as you can. Keep
squeezing for a moment...
Then let your hands go flop,
like a flippety floppety rabbit.

Breathe in and squeeze
your tummy tight. Hold it
in for a moment... Then let it
go flop, like a flippety floppety rabbit.

Squeeze your tail – if you don't
have a tail, you can squeeze
your bottom and legs.
Keep squeezing for a moment...
Then let go, like
a flippety floppety rabbit.

Scrunch up your toes tight.
Keep them scrunched for a moment...

Then let them go flop, like a...
FLIPPETY FLOPPETY RABBIT!

THINGS TO TALK ABOUT
(FOR GROWN-UPS)

Sometimes adults think they know what's best, but often the most helpful thing will be for the child to see that you are really listening to them. Ask the child about:

• **How they reacted initially.**

Everyone reacts in different ways to shock. Reassure them that however they reacted, it was their body's normal reaction to an unusual situation.

- ## How they feel now.

  Are there ways in which the child's behaviour has changed since the event? If so, try to understand the thoughts and feelings behind the behaviour. Just listening to what they tell you can make a big difference. If they have trouble describing how they feel, they can tell you by pointing at the different feelings on the last page of the story.

- ## Finding other ways to let their feelings out.

  As well as talking, think about other ways they can express how they feel e.g. drawing, music, play, dance, sports, etc.

- **Making a plan, if they want to.**

The first step is to give them plenty of time. If, after some time, the 'strange things that are happening' persist (e.g. nightmares, never wanting to be alone and so on), you may want to help them make a plan. Ask them what makes them feel happy and safe, and plan to do more of it. Ask them what they need from you – do they have questions about what happened, or do they need help with a certain activity?

- **Doing the Flippety Floppety Rabbit.**

Do this relaxation exercise with them a few times so they can see how it works and use it when they're on their own.

Also, look after yourself! Children pick up the feelings of grown-ups around them. Try to recognise ways you may also have been affected by the incident and find someone to talk to or make a plan of your own. You can get also help and advice from your doctor or agencies like Victim Support.